IT'S TIME TO COMB YOUR HAIR

By: Tanisha Singleton Thompson,
Veriteady Thompson and Klere Kado Thompson

Illustration by: Jamil Burton

©2021 by Tanisha Singleton Thompson
ALL RIGHTS RESERVED

All rights reserved. No part of this publication may be reproduced, distributed, or transmitted in any form or by any means, including photocopying, recording, or other electronic or mechanical methods, without the prior written permission of the publisher, except in the case of brief quotations embodied in critical reviews and certain other noncommercial uses permitted by copyright law. For permission requests, contact Tanisha Singleton Thompson at singleton127@yahoo.com

ISBN: 978-0-578-87445-6

©2021 by Tanisha Singleton Thompson
ALL RIGHTS RESERVED

All rights reserved. No part of this publication may be reproduced, distributed, or transmitted in any form or by any means, including photocopying, recording, or other electronic or mechanical methods, without the prior written permission of the publisher, except in the case of brief quotations embodied in critical reviews and certain other noncommercial uses permitted by copyright law. For permission requests, contact Tanisha Singleton Thompson at singleton127@yahoo.com

ISBN: 978-0-578-87445-6

IT'S TIME TO COMB YOUR HAIR

By: Tanisha Singleton Thompson,
Veriteady Thompson and Klere Kado Thompson

Illustration by: Jamil Burton

Illustrator: Jamil Burton

Book Interior Designer: Zuliesuivie Ball

Editors: Zuliesuivie Ball and Carolyn Ball

DEDICATION

Veriteady and Klere Kado you are my loves. I thank you for being such wonderful daughters and always being great supporters and helpers in everything that I do. Spending time with you, while doing your hair, can be challenging sometimes, but I love the time we spend together! I will always love and cherish the moments we spend with each other.

Love,
Mommy

SPECIAL THANKS!

To my husband, Rahim Thompson

To my parents Betty and Mantson Singleton

To my little cousin Victoria Lynn Chestine

To my wonderful and supportive family and friends!

Today is the third Saturday of the month and it is such a special day, Healthy Hair Flair Day. This is the day when Mama detangles, conditions, moisturizes and combs Alia and her younger sister, Halima's hair.

"Alia! It's time to comb your hair," Mama shouts. Alia peeps down the stairs and notices Mama carrying her favorite pink plushy chair, the detangling lotion, and her three combs! Alia dashes down the stairs and hides behind the living room couch!

"Oh no, Mama! Please don't comb my hair today!" Alia replies. Mama walks over to the couch. "Alia, I can see your hair so come out from behind there. You know today is our special hair day, Healthy Hair Flair Day!" Mama says. "This is our time to bond, talk with one another and comb your hair." She then takes Alia by the hand and begins to walk her over to her favorite pink plushy chair.

"Wait Mama, I know it's Healthy Hair Flair Day, but can it be canceled? I do not like my hair combed Mama! When you comb my hair it hurts so bad it makes me feel really, really Mis-er-a-ble !" whined Alia.

"Miserable? Really Alia, I'm sorry you feel that way, but it's time to comb your hair," Mama said.

Alia took her hand away, ran over to her pink plushy chair, covered her face and began to whine even harder. "Mama, noooo, nooooo, noooooo! Don't comb my hair!" Alia screamed. "Alia, please settle down. If I don't comb your hair, it's going to become tangled, matted and unmanageable, and then what are you going to do?" Mama asks.

Alia suddenly got quiet and removed her hands from her face. Her eyes began to sparkle and a great big grin appeared across her face. Alia immediately jumped up, ran into the kitchen and began singing, "I got an idea! I got an idea! I got an ideaaaa!!!

Alia runs past her sister, Halima, and shuffles through the kitchen cabinets. "Sister, what are you looking for?" said Halima. "You will see. Just wait!" exclaimed Alia. Alia grabs a big brown paper bag and struggles to place it over all of her tangled hair.

"Sister, I don't think this is a good idea. Mama is not going to let you wear a bag to cover your hair," said Halima. "How do you know? Have you tried it?" said Alia. Halima shook her head slowly to say no.
"I didn't think so! So help me put my hair inside the bag," said Alia.

The two sisters pushed and tucked and rolled and stuffed. "This is not easy sister. How are you going to do this every day?" grunted Halima. "Don't you worry about it. Let's just get the rest of my hair in and we can figure the rest out later." Alia said breathing heavily. They pushed, tucked, rolled and stuffed some more until the bag was able to sit just right on Alia's head.

"Tah dah! I look perfect!" shouted Alia. "With this bag on my head, Mama will surely cancel Healthy Hair Flair Day!" Alia was so excited about what she accomplished. Alia darted out of the kitchen and ran straight into Mama, who was on her way to the kitchen to get her!

"Whoa! Alia watch where you are going," said Mama. "Sorry, but look at what I did! I recycled this bag and created a hat big enough for my hair, and no one will notice if my hair is tangled, matted or unmanageable!"

Mama chuckled and said, "Alia you can barely see. Are you going to wear this bag covering your face the entire day?" "Why not?" Alia replies. "I'll have more time to play if we cancel Healthy Hair Flair Day." Mama shakes her head and said, "Alia, please come and sit down. It's time to comb your hair!" Mama removes the bag and places a green all purpose comb in Alia's hair and Alia walks back very angrily to her pink plushy chair.

Alia sat down with her arms folded tight and said, "I really don't like getting my hair combed! I don't like it! I really don't like it! These combs hurt so bad and it makes me feel really, really sad," pouted Alia.

While Alia waited for Mama to return back to the couch, she thought of an idea and scurried out of the living room and up the stairs. Alia screamed, "I'll be right back! Just wait right there!" Mama screamed back, " Hurry up Alia, it's time to comb your hair!" Mama and Halima waited for Alia to return.

When Alia came back, she had a big surprise on her head! It was Mama's wig! "Mama, we can cancel Healthy Hair Flair Day for sure! I found a solution! Mama and Halima bursted out with laughter! "Sister, you can't be serious?" said Halima. "Oh yes I am! I look amazing!" shouted Alia.

"Alia, you are such a silly girl. First of all, that's my hair unit! Second, the hair is not even covering your whole head. So please, please, take it back to my room and come sit down in your pink plushy chair! It's time to comb your hair!" laughed Mama.

Alia came back from Mama's room and sat still enough for Mama to go from section to section to apply the detangling lotion and a moisturizer to Alia's hair, but when Mama started to loosen up her curls with her fingers, Alia began to tighten her body and started complaining. "Ouch Mama, this really hurts! Are you almost done combing my hair?"

"Alia I am just getting started. Just hold still and let me run my fingers through your curls. Sometimes I have to use my fingers to loosen the roots so it can make the combing easier. If you concentrate on things that make you happy, this process will go so much faster. So close your eyes and share with me, what a perfect day for you would be?" asked Mama.

Alia closed her eyes and smiled so happily and said, "a perfect day for me would be to cancel Healthy Hair Flair Day! There would be no combs in my hair at all!" Alia said excitedly. "Oh really?" said Mama. "Yeah, I will go outside and let the wind blow in my tangled hair, and I would play in the sun all day." said Alia. " Wow, all day? That's a long time," said Mama.

"I know! It will be so great! I would play my favorite game of hide and seek. While my sister and friend goes hide, I would jump rope and count with my eyes closed." said Alia. " You can jump with your eyes closed?" Mama said. "Yeah Mama, I'm a pro!" said Alia. "Ok pro!" shouted Halima and Mama.

While Alia continued to talk, Mama parted Alia's hair with a rat-tail comb and then detangled it with a wide-tooth comb, nice and gentle, from ends to roots. Alia did not move at all because she was so focused on telling Mama and Halima all the details about her "Perfect Day." "Sister, that sounds like a great day!" said Halima. "It sure does." agreed Mama. "Yeah it really would be an awesome day if Mama would cancel Healthy Hair Flair Day!" said Alia.

"Alia, if I canceled Healthy Hair Flair Day, I wouldn't be able to spend this special time with you. I wouldn't be able to hear your awesome stories or experience all the creative ways you try to get out of combing your hair. I wouldn't be able to get all the tangles out and showcase your beautiful curls. I wouldn't be able to moisturize and add that special shine. Combing your hair is very special to me, and when you keep still I am able to get done in a short time," said Mama. "Mama I did not know that Healthy Hair Flair Day was so special to you. I will keep still right now until you are through!" said Alia.

Mama takes the rat tail comb, parts Alia's hair in the middle, and smooths her edges down with the teeth of the comb. "I am finished!" Mama said. "Wow Mama! Already? I just sat down!" Alia said. "It doesn't take long if you just keep still when it's time to comb your hair." Mama said. Alia jumped out of her favorite pink plushy chair and ran down the hallway and into the bathroom to check out her hair in the mirror!

Alia smiled as she admired her beautiful untangled, moisturized and manageable hair. "Thank you Mama so much for detangling my hair. Now I can style it however I want! I can wear it just like this, up in a ponytail or in two-strand twists. I can add a headband, clips or bows. Next time, I am going to sit still on Healthy Hair Flair Day when it's time to comb my hair!" shouted Alia. "Sure you will Alia, you say that every third Saturday of the month!" laughed Mama.

THE END!

Made in the USA
Middletown, DE
19 April 2021